JOURNEY CAKE, HO!

JOURNEY CAKE,
HO!

By Ruth Sawyer

Illustrated by
Robert McCloskey

New York · THE VIKING PRESS

Copyright 1953 by Ruth Sawyer and Robert McCloskey
All rights reserved
Viking Seafarer edition issued in 1970 by The Viking Press, Inc.
625 Madison Avenue, New York, N.Y. 10022
Distributed in Canada by
The Macmillan Company of Canada Limited
Library of Congress catalog card number: 53–3366
Pic Bk 1. Animals—Stories
2. Folklore—U.S.

Printed in U.S.A.
SBN 670–05036–9
2   3   4   5   74   73   72

JOURNEY CAKE, HO!

There were three of them:
      the old woman, Merry;
           the old man, Grumble;

and Johnny, the bound-out boy.
They lived in a log cabin, t'other side of Tip Top Mountain.

The old woman took care of the wool; she carded and spun and knit it. She laid the fire, tended the griddle, churned the butter, and sang at her work. The song she liked best ran this-wise:

"Ho, for a Journey Cake—
Quick on a griddle bake!
Sugar and salt it,
Turn it and brown it,
Johnny, come eat it with milk for your tea."

The old man tended the garden patch, sheared the sheep, milked the cow, felled the trees, sawed the logs, and grumbled at his work. The grumble he liked best was:

"A bother, a pest!
All work and no rest!
Come winter, come spring,
Life's a nettlesome thing."

And what about Johnny? He split the kindling, filled the
woodbox, lugged the water, fed the creatures, fished the

brook, and whistled at his work. One tune was as fine as another to Johnny.

Their whole world lay close about them. There were the garden patch, the brook, the logging road that ran down to the valley where the villagers lived, and the spruce woods.

On the tallest tree sat Raucus, the sentinel crow, watching and waiting to caw when surprise or trouble was near.

Nothing happened for a long, long time. They lived snug, like rabbits in their burrow. Then—

One night a fox carried off the hens. "Caw, caw!" called
the crow. But it was too late. The next night a wolf carried

off the sheep. "Caw, caw, caw!" called the crow. But it was
too late.

There came a day when the pig wandered off and got himself lost. Last of all the cow fell into the brook and broke her leg.

All that day the crow cawed and cawed and cawed.

That night the old woman said, shaking her head, "Trouble has come. The meal chest is low, the bin is near empty. What will feed two will not feed three."

The old man grumbled and said, "Johnny, 'tis likely you'll be leaving us on the morrow and finding yourself a new master and a new ma'm."

The next morning by sunup the old woman had run together a piece of sacking and put straps to it, to hold Johnny's belongings—a knife, some gum from the spruce trees, his shoes and a washing-cloth. On top went the Journey Cake that had been baked for him. It was large, round, and

crusty-hard. "Now be off with you!" said the old man, grumbling. "What must be, must be."

"Off with you—and luck follow after," said the old woman sadly.

Johnny said nothing at all. He left his whistle behind him and took the logging road down to the valley.

Right foot, left foot, right foot, left foot. He was halfway

down and more when the straps on his sacking bag broke loose. Out bounced the Journey Cake.

It bumped and it bumped; it rolled over and over. Down the road it went, and how it hollered!

"Journey Cake, ho!
Journey Cake, hi!
Catch me and eat me
As I roll by!"

Away and away rolled the Journey Cake. Away and away
ran Johnny.

Faster and faster. They passed a field full of cows. A
brindle cow tossed her head and took after them. She mooed:
"At running I'll beat you.
I'll catch you and eat you!"

Faster and faster, faster and faster! They passed a pond full
of ducks.   "Journey Cake, ho!
               Journey Cake, hi!
               Catch me and eat me
               As I roll by!"

A white duck spread her wings, and away and away she
went after them, quacking:

"At flying I'll beat you.

I'll catch and I'll eat you!"

Faster and faster, faster and faster! They came to a meadow where sheep were grazing. A white sheep and a black sheep took after them

                Now they were through the valley

and the road began to climb. Slower and slower rolled the
Journey Cake. Slower and slower ran Johnny, the brindle
cow, the white duck, and the two sheep.

"Journey Cake, hi!

The journey is long.

Catch me and eat me
As I roll along."
They passed a wallows. A spotted pig heard and came
a-grunting.

They passed a barnyard, and a flock of red hens flew over
the stump fence, squawking.

Slower and s·l·o·w·e·r,   higher and higher.

At last they came to a mountain pasture where a gray
donkey was feeding. Now the Journey Cake was huffing and
puffing:

"Journey Cake, hi!
The journey is long.

C-c-catch me and eat me—
As I roll along."
The donkey was fresh. He kicked up his heels and brayed:
"I'll show I can beat you.
I'll catch you and eat you."

Higher went the road. Slower and slower, slower and
slower rolled the Journey Cake—t'other side of Tip Top
Mountain. Slower and slower and slower, slower and slower
came the procession with Johnny at the head. Huffing and
puffing, they circled the spruce woods. From his perch on

the tallest tree, Raucus, the crow, let out his surprise warning:
"Caw, caw, caw!"

Johnny heard. He stopped, all of a quickness. There was
the brook; there was the garden patch; there was the log
cabin.

He was home again. The Journey Cake had brought him
to the end of his journey!

The Journey Cake spun around twice and fell flat. "I'm
all of a tucker!" it hollered.

"We're all of a tucker," cried the others. The red hens found a house waiting for them. The cow found her tether-rope; the pig found a sty; the duck found a brook; the sheep found a place for grazing, and the donkey walked himself into the shed.

The old woman came a-running.

The old man came a-running.

Johnny hugged them hard. He found his whistle again and took up the merriest tune. "Wheee—ew, wheee—ew!" he whistled. He hopped first on right foot, then on left foot.

When he had his breath he said, "Journey Cake did it. Journey Cake fetched me and the cow and the white duck and the black and white sheep and the flock of red hens and the pig and the gray donkey. Now they are all yours!"

The old man forgot his best grumble. The old woman
picked up the Journey Cake and went inside to freshen it
up on the griddle. She went, singing the song she liked best:

"Warm up the Journey Cake;
From now on it's Johnny Cake.
Johnny, come eat it
With milk for your tea!"